D0126069

W9. BMH.578

STAR WARS

LUKE AND THE LOST JEDI TEMPLE

ADAPTED BY **JASON FRY**

BASED ON **WEAPON OF A JEDI** BY JASON FRY

ILLUSTRATED BY **PILOT STUDIO**

Printed in the United States of America

First Paperback Edition, November 2016

1 3 5 7 9 10 8 6 4 2

Library of Congress Control Number on file

FAC-029261-16260

ISBN 978-1-4847-0505-6

Visit the official *Star Wars* website at: www.starwars.com.

SUSTAINABLE FORESTRY INITIATIVE

Certified Sourcing

www.sfiprogram.org

SFI-01415

Disney

LUCASFILM

PRESS

LOS ANGELES · NEW YORK

LUKE SKYWALKER WAS IN TROUBLE!

His Y-wing fighter had been damaged in a battle with the Empire, and he needed to find a safe place to land—and fast!

As he flew low over the jungle planet of Devaron, something interesting caught his eye. It was the ruins of a temple. The mysterious energy field known as the Force told him the temple was important.

Luke was traveling with his faithful droids, C-3PO and R2-D2. C-3PO feared Imperial stormtroopers would be waiting for them wherever they landed. But Luke sensed that he needed to visit the ruins.

Once on the ground, there was no sign of Imperial troops. A mechanic named Kivas and his daughter, Farnay, agreed to fix Luke's fighter while he and the droids explored.

The nearby village was bustling with life.

Luke soon found guides who were eager to take him hunting for creatures called pikhrons.

But Luke didn't want to go hunting.

He wanted to visit the ruined temple.

The locals refused to help him. They said the temple was forbidden.

Only one guide would take Luke into the jungle. He was an alien named Sarco Plank. Farnay warned Luke that people who traveled with Sarco didn't return. Luke appreciated Farnay's warning, but he had no choice. The Force was calling him to the temple.

Sarco, Luke, and the droids mounted beasts called happabores and rode off into the jungle. On their journey Sarco noticed Luke's lightsaber—the weapon of a Jedi Knight. Luke didn't want Sarco to know he could feel the Force, so he pretended that he didn't know how to use the lightsaber.

When they reached the temple, R2-D2 detected Imperial probe droids floating among the ruins. The Empire clearly didn't want visitors.

Through the Force, Luke sensed a secret cave high on a cliff above an old riverbed. That would be their way in! Leaving Sarco behind, Luke and the droids climbed into the cave and walked down a dark, twisty passageway.

When Luke reached the temple, he found it in ruins. Statues of ancient Jedi were scattered in pieces on the ground. But at its center, Luke found a battered but beautiful courtyard. He heard a voice inside his head. It was his old teacher, Obi-Wan Kenobi!

Obi-Wan had taught Luke a little about the Force before the evil Darth Vader struck him down in a lightsaber duel. Obi-Wan was gone but could still speak to Luke through the Force. He told Luke that the Force had guided him to the temple. There Luke would learn to open his mind to the Force's teachings.

Luke took in his surroundings.

At the top of a nearby pillar was a lever. Luke tried and tried to use the Force to move it, but it wouldn't budge. He didn't know what to do.

Then a beautiful, brightly colored insect landed on Luke's arm. He heard Obi-Wan's voice again, urging him to feel the Force everywhere.

Through the Force, Luke focused on the lever once more, and it moved!

A metal orb emerged from the pillar. It was like the remote that Obi-Wan had once used to train Luke. Luke ignited his lightsaber and tried to command the Force. C-3PO and R2-D2 stood by, watching Luke as he dueled with the device that zipped through the air and fired stinging laser beams.

When the orb backed away, Luke smiled. He had passed the test!

Then two more remotes emerged! It was impossible to keep track of three devices at once! Luke almost felt like he'd be better off fighting blind, the way Obi-Wan had made him train aboard the *Millennium Falcon*.

Luke realized that Obi-Wan had been trying to teach him to trust the Force instead of his senses. Jedi Knights didn't guide the Force but let it guide *them*.

Luke took a deep breath and tried again. This time, he let the Force direct his movements.

The three training remotes flew into attack mode. Luke spun left and right, his lightsaber flashing. He fought for hours, and not one laser bolt got through his defenses!

Suddenly, a laser blast knocked Luke off his feet! But it wasn't a remote shooting at him. The Empire's stormtroopers had found him, and they had captured Farnay! She must have followed him to keep an eye on Sarco.

Luke was outnumbered and about to surrender when Sarco Plank emerged from behind the ruins. The guide was holding a crackling electrostaff and was there to help Luke!

Fighting side by side, Luke and Sarco defeated the Imperial soldiers.

But just as the last stormtrooper fell . . .

. . . Sarco turned on Luke and Farnay. He was much more dangerous than Luke realized. Sarco was planning to steal Luke's lightsaber, melt down the droids, and loot any Jedi treasures left in the temple.

Sarco threw a grenade into the air, and it exploded with a brilliant flash and a thunderclap. The impact knocked Luke down and left him unable to see or hear.

Luke tried to fight Sarco, but he was facing the wrong way. As Farnay and the droids watched in horror, Sarco raised his electrostaff and walked slowly toward Luke.

Luke started to panic, but then he heard Obi-Wan's voice, reminding him that while his eyes and ears could deceive him, the Force was all-seeing.

Moving with incredible speed and using the Force to guide him, Luke spun into action! He swung the blade of his lightsaber into Sarco's chest, knocking the alien back. Sarco staggered and fell into a deep pit in the courtyard. Luke had defeated him for now, but the alien would surely rise again.

Farnay and the droids rushed over to Luke, but there was no time to celebrate. TIE fighters shrieked overhead. Luke, Farnay, and the droids knew they had to flee. Luke stopped for a moment in the ruins of the lost Jedi temple. Lifting his lightsaber, Luke swore he would become a Jedi Knight . . . perhaps even the greatest Jedi of all!